DAISY'S REALITY SHOW ADVENTURE

A Dog Tale

Carol Wallace

Illustrations: Carol Wallace

Table of Contents

For more fun, visit the book's Web site:
www.DaisyDogEnterprises.com

FOX TERRIER NETWORK

BREAKING NEWS

Daisy has postponed her national book tour in order to make appearances at town halls and universities across the country to "let her bark be heard." She's been spending her senior years on a Montana ranch after leaving Hollywood, trading her stilettos for cowboy boots and chilling out, but came out of retirement knowing she had to be the calming voice of reason and display her signature teeth-baring to those who have been showing the disobedient behavior she's been watching on TV reports.

"Someone has to do it," she wistfully barks.

Her first stop will be D.C., where she arranged a cordial muzzle-to-muzzle meeting between President Don Dog (referenced in her book before his election), Congressional Representative Maxine Water Dog and a comedian named Kathy, a Petit Basset Griffon who fell prey to Small Dog Syndrome.

AMERICA'S ULTIMATE COMFORT DOG PRESENTS HER LIFE STORY TO THE DISHEARTENED AND DISILLUSIONED IN THESE TUMULTUOUS TIMES;

(ESPECIALLY MILLENNIALS AND HOLLYWOOD CELEBRITIES). JOIN DAISY AS SHE TRANSCENDS HER HUMBLE BEGINNINGS IN A PUPPY FARM TO RIDE THE REALITY SHOW CIRCUIT AND BASK IN THE HOLLYWOOD SPOTLIGHT (WITH A LITTLE POLITICKING THROWN IN AS WELL), ENCOUNTERING TERRIER-ABLE OBSTACLES ALONG THE WAY.

READ ABOUT HER APPEARANCES WITH SIMON HOWL AND STEVEN TERRIER ON *AMERICAN HOWLER*, AND THE LUMINARIES ON *PROJECT DOGRUN*, *TOP MUTT CHEF* AND *RETRIEVER*. CRY ALONG WITH HER WHEN SHE IS DOGNAPPED BY THE PUGNACIOUS FILMMAKER-POLITICAL ACTIVIST MICHAEL, "PUGGY" PUGNOSE; AND AS SHE ENDURES THE MEAN-SPIRITED FAKE NEWS STORIES BY TABLOID REPORTERS.

APPLAUD HER BRAVE DECISION TO SEEK COUNSELING FROM THE GREAT DANE, DR. PHIL MCGROWL TO RECOVER FROM HER DEVASTATION. JOIN DAISY ON HER FOX TERRIER NETWORK PROGRAM, *THE RANT AND PANT SHOW*, WHERE SHE HOSTS THE CLASSIC BARKFEST BETWEEN THE BELLICOSE ALASKAN

HUSKY, SARAH GROWLIN' AND A DOUR LITTLE BARKER, ELIZABETH, A CANARANIAN WARREN HOUND.

ENJOY THE LESSONS SHE IMPARTS AS A SENIOR DOG, WHO HAS SEEN HERSELF GO FROM CREAM PUFF TO PUMA. DAISY HOPES HER STORY WILL ENCOURAGE HER READERS TO EMERGE FROM THEIR SAFE, COMFY SPACES, DRY THEIR TEARS, AND FACE THE TRIALS AND TRIBULATIONS OF REAL LIFE WITH VIGOR, ACCEPTANCE AND SELF-RESPECT.

DAISY HOPES HER READERS WILL HAVE FUN MATCHING UP THE THINLY-DISGUISED CHARACTERS IN HER BOOK WITH REAL-LIFE ACTORS, MUSICIANS, AND POLITICIANS. "LEVITY IS THE BEST MEDICINE FOR A BROKEN HEART," DAISY YAPS. "WE ALL NEED TO BARK-LAUGH AT OURSELVES NOW AND THEN."

Leg I

From Country Dog

To Discovered Dog

Performing I'm In A Canine State Of Mind

DAISY WAS A RAT TERRIER WHOSE LIFE
WAS ABOUT TO TAKE AN UNEXPECTED AND

EXCITING TURN. BORN ON A PUPPY FARM IN RURAL SOUTHEASTERN PENNSYLVANIA, SHE HAD LIVED THERE FOR SIX MONTHS, ANXIOUSLY AWAITING THE TIME WHEN SOMEONE FROM THE STEADY STREAM OF BOSS DOGS, LOOKING FOR HELP, WOULD DISCOVER HER POTENTIAL AND GIVE HER A JOB.

IN THIS WORLD OF DOGDOM EXISTED A HIERARCHY: THE HAVES AND THE HAVE-NOTS... PUREBRED DOGS POSSESSING GREAT WEALTH AND PRIVILEGE, AND THE WORKING CLASS, COMPRISED OF MIXED-BREED DOGS OF LESSER FINANCIAL AND SOCIAL STATURE. SOCIETY FAVORED THE UPPER CLASS, AND THE WORKING DOGS MUST EARN THEIR KEEP. FIRST THEY HAD TO WORK OFF THE FEE PAID FOR THEM, AND THEN WERE SALARIED, ENABLING THEM THE OPPORTUNITY TO SOMEDAY ACQUIRE THEIR OWN WEALTH AND BUSINESSES. THIS DIDN'T HAPPEN OFTEN, BUT IT WAS POSSIBLE.

THE DOG FARM RESIDENTS CONSISTED OF MOSTLY MIXED-BREED CANINES, BUT INCLUDED A FEW PUREBREDS LIKE DAISY, WHO HAD PHYSICAL DEFORMITIES. THERE WERE ALSO SOME MEMBERS OF PUREBRED BREEDS LIVING

THERE WHO HAD FALLEN OUT OF FAVOR WITHIN THE UPPER-CRUST POPULACE. IF THESE DOG FARM DWELLERS HAD ANY CHANCE OF ELEVATING THEIR SOCIAL STATUS, THEY'D HAVE TO WORK HARD AT IT. NOTHING WAS FREE — NO TRUST FUNDS FOR THEM. THESE CANINES LIVED A DOG-EAT-DOG EXISTENCE.

CLIENTS COMING TO THE DOG FARM HAD VARIOUS REASONS FOR SELECTING CERTAIN DOGS. SOME CANINES, ESPECIALLY DOWAGERS, LIKED THE IDEA OF MENTORING DOGS TO TURN THEM INTO IMAGES OF THEMSELVES...OR THEY WANTED COMPANIONS...WHILE OTHERS SIMPLY WANTED GUARD DOGS, HARD LABORERS AND, IN SOME INSTANCES, JUST SHOW-OFF DOGS. TO HAVE A MIXED-BREED DOG WORKING FOR YOU WAS A STATUS SYMBOL FOR THE PUREBRED VARIETY. THE ORPHANS AT THE FARM KNEW THIS AND WERE ALWAYS HOPING FOR A KIND AND CARING OWNER.

DIMINUTIVE IN SIZE, BUT MIGHTY IN PRESENCE, DAISY POSSESSED A DISARMING PERSONALITY AND EXTRAORDINARY WARMTH AND KINDNESS. BUT DAISY HAD A BIRTH DEFECT THAT WAS A TURNOFF FOR THOSE

WHO WERE LOOKING FOR THE PERFECT CANINE. THE TIP OF HER LEFT EAR WAS BENT OVER, AND A DARK PURPLE BIRTHMARK, RESEMBLING A DAISY, STOOD OUT IN THE MIDDLE OF THAT TURNED-OVER AREA. IT DIDN'T SEEM TO MATTER THAT, IN ADDITION TO HER ENDEARING INNER-DOG, SHE WAS QUITE ATTRACTIVE PHYSICALLY, WITH A SLIM, MUSCULAR BODY AND A FACE GRACED WITH LOVELY BLACK AND BROWN MARKINGS, LARGE BROWN SOULFUL EYES, AND PERFECTLY SHAPED EYEBROWS. THE ONLY THING THE BOSS DOGS EVER NOTICED WAS HER IMPERFECTION.

SHE WAS THE BUTT OF JOKES FROM THE OTHER WORKING DOGS AS WELL. "DOG-EAR," THEY'D CALL HER — AND THERE WERE SNIDE WHISPERS AND EYE ROLLING WHEN SHE ENTERED A ROOM. HAD IT NOT BEEN FOR HER FRIEND, WOOLLY, A TIBETAN SPANIEL WHO WORKED AT THE FARM AS A PHYSICIAN ASSISTANT, DAISY WOULD HAVE BEEN COMPLETELY DEVASTATED. IT WAS GOOD HAVING AN ASSERTIVE FRIEND LIKE HIM WHO TOLD IT THE WAY IT WAS.

"Don't pay attention to them," Woolly barked. "It's what's inside that matters. Someday they will see that. Those cruel mutts are just shallow."

Woolly's support and friendship helped Daisy get through the inhumane treatment, and she was able to focus on her dream: being of service to others. While most of the dogs at the farm spent lazy days lying on the couch, socializing, occasionally chasing squirrels, and barking at the UPS dog, Daisy used her free time to volunteer as a cook and art instructor at Sheltie's Cat Shelter.

The Arteest

SHE WAS ALSO A FREQUENT VISITOR AT THE GERIATRIC DOG HOME WHERE SHE ENJOYED TEACHING OLD DOGS NEW TRICKS. HER BREED OF DOG HAD A TRAIT, A HIGH-PITCHED HOWL, THAT MADE HER A NATURAL TO WORK WITH THE HEARING IMPAIRED. AND, IN DAISY'S CASE, SHE HAD PERFECT PITCH ALONG WITH TALENT AND STYLE, WHICH PLEASED THE SENIOR DOGS TO NO END. ONE DAY SHE WOULD SHIMMY AND SHAKE WHILE BELTING OUT *YOU AIN'T NOTHIN' BUT A HOUND DOG* — ANOTHER TIME SHE'D DRAPE HERSELF OVER THE PIANO AND SING, IN A SULTRY CABARET-STYLE, *WHY DID I CHEW SHOES?*

ONCE A MONTH THE FARM HELD A "*GET TO KNOW OUR CANINES*" OPEN HOUSE FUNCTION, WHERE CLIENTS WOULD COME TO INSPECT THE DOGS. DAISY KNEW THE DRILL, AND EVEN THOUGH SHE ALWAYS TRIED HER BEST TO GET POTENTIAL BUYERS TO SHOW INTEREST IN HER, SHE WAS LIKELY TO BE DISAPPOINTED AGAIN AND AGAIN.

EVERY TIME SHE WAS LEFT STANDING IN THE ROOM AT THE END OF THE DAY, STILL HOLDING THE FLOWER IN HER TEETH SHE HAD

READY TO GIVE TO THE BOSS DOG WHO CHOSE HER. SHE ALWAYS WATCHED WITH TEARS IN HER EYES AS SHE WAS BYPASSED IN FAVOR OF OTHER PUPPIES WHO WERE WHISKED AWAY TO REWARDING JOBS AND NEW LIVES. THEN SHE'D TURN AND SLOWLY WALK BACK UP THE STAIRS TO HER ROOM AND STARE OUT THE WINDOW FOR HOURS, WONDERING HOW SHE COULD MAKE ANYONE SEE HER POTENTIAL. BUT DAISY HAD GREAT PERSEVERANCE AND SOMETHING INSIDE TOLD HER TO KEEP TRYING AND NOT GIVE UP.

Yearning For Adventure

Daisy seldom felt welcome at the evening dog activities. Instead, she stayed in her room watching Reality TV programs and, in no time, she was hooked. Once she started, she couldn't stop. It was an attraction-repulsion sort of thing. Woolly was bitten by the same flea, and soon they were yipping and yapping about the stars and happenings on *Cate Without Mate & Her Litter Of Eight*, *The Real Housedogs Of New Jersey*, *Keeping Up With The Cur-Dachshunds*, *The Biggest Bowser*, *Little Miss Puppy Princess*, *The Tail-Waggers Next Door*, *Dogs Behaving Badly*, *Bark Tank*, *The Lab Five*, and other popular programs.

"Did you see Taleasha, the Segugio Italiano, tip her food bowl on *The Real Housedogs Of New Jersey*?" Daisy barked.

"Yes, she was sooo out of control! Someone oughta tighten her leash," Woolly woofed. "She needs a behaviorist."

"AND I THOUGHT DOGAROSA CROSSED THE LINE ON *DOGS BEHAVING BADLY* — THOSE JACK RUSSELL TERRIERS CAN SURE DO SOME DAMAGE WHEN THEY'RE BORED," DAISY YIPPED.

ONE CHILLY AUTUMN DAY, DAISY WAS RETURNING FROM THE CAT SHELTER AND OVERHEARD A CONVERSATION BETWEEN THE OWNERS OF THE PUPPY FARM AS SHE PASSED THEIR OFFICE DOOR. THEY WERE DISCUSSING HER!

"DAISY'S BEEN HERE MORE THAN ENOUGH TIME TO ATTRACT A BUYER. I THINK WE SHOULD GIVE HER JUST ONE MORE WEEK, AND IF SOMEONE DOESN'T PICK HER, WE'LL HAVE TO PUT HER DOWN," BARKED GUS, A BELLICOSE BULL TERRIER.

DAISY BROKE INTO A PANT WHEN SHE HEARD THIS DISTRESSING NEWS, BUT SHE MUSTERED HER NATURAL FEISTINESS AND BECAME DETERMINED TO PUT HERSELF IN THE SPOTLIGHT AT THE NEXT OPEN HOUSE. SOME OF HER RELATIVES HAD BEEN CIRCUS PERFORMERS, SO SHE KNEW IT WAS IN HER GENES!

Daisy stitched up a cute costume to wear with a matching beret to conceal her ears. The big night came, and when the showroom was filled, Daisy made her grand entrance. As planned, Woolly shined a flashlight on Daisy, and her performance began. She jumped on a table, grabbed the microphone, and belted out *I'm In A Canine State Of Mind*, followed by a little soft shoe, and ending with three quick back flips.

The crowd was going crazy, baying and woof-woofing...until the final flip loosened her hat and exposed her blemished ear. Silence swept over the room as everyone turned uncomfortably and walked away.

Daisy thought she was a dead dog — until Woolly tapped her on the flank and pointed his nose across the room. She noticed a Scottish Terrier watching her as he talked to Gus. The two canines walked toward Daisy and her heart began to pitter-patter furiously. She could not believe her good fortune when she was

TOLD SHE'D BE LEAVING THAT VERY NIGHT FOR HER NEW HOME WITH THE DISTINGUISHED-LOOKING MR. RUFUS.

DAISY RACED UPSTAIRS TO PACK HER SUITCASE AND LEARNED THAT WOOLLY HAD BEEN NABBED THAT NIGHT AS WELL. HE WAS OFF TO LIVE WITH A NICE YOUNG FAMILY OF IRISH SETTERS, THE O'SYCAMORAS, WHERE HE WOULD BE A COMPANION FOR THEIR GRANDMOTHER, MOLLY. DAISY AND WOOLLY PASSED EACH OTHER IN THE HALL AND SHARED A CONGRATULATORY HIGH PAW-SLAP...TWO FRIENDS ABOUT TO EMBARK ON EXCITING NEW ADVENTURES.

DAISY AND HER NEW EMPLOYER ENGAGED IN THE CANINE RITUAL OF SNIFFING AND LICKING IN ORDER TO GET TO KNOW EACH OTHER BEFORE LEAVING THE FARM. DAISY IMMEDIATELY SENSED A COOL RESERVE IN MR. RUFUS. SOMETHING DIDN'T SMELL QUITE RIGHT — BUT DAISY, ALWAYS THE OPTIMIST, PUSHED THE NEGATIVE THOUGHTS OUT OF HER MIND WITH DOGGED DETERMINATION.

MR. RUFUS GROWLED, "LET'S GO," AND DAISY SUBMISSIVELY FOLLOWED BEHIND HIM. WHEN SHE STARTED TO HOP INTO THE PASSENGER

SEAT, HE SNARLED AT HER AND JERKED HIS HEAD TOWARD THE REAR OF THE CAR. "GET IN THE BACK SEAT!"

DAISY CLIMBED INTO THE REAR COMPARTMENT AND MUTTERED UNDER HER BREATH, "WHATEVER!"

THE DRIVE WAS A QUIET ONE WITH NO COMMUNICATION BETWEEN THE TWO CANINES. WHEN THE CAR TURNED INTO THE DRIVEWAY OF A BEAUTIFUL VICTORIAN INN AND SHE SAW THE ILLUMINATED SIGN, "RUFUS'S BED & BISCUIT," DAISY BROKE OUT WITH YELPS OF JOY! IT HAD BEEN DAISY'S LIFE-LONG DREAM TO LIVE IN AN ESTABLISHMENT LIKE THIS. SHE THOUGHT ABOUT THE MANY THINGS SHE COULD DO TO HELP WITH HER CONSIDERABLE SKILLS...ASSISTING IN THE PREPARATION OF MEALS, DECORATING GUEST ROOMS BY SEWING CURTAINS, BEDSPREADS, AND CUSHION COVERS...PERHAPS EVEN SERENADING GUESTS IN THE EVENINGS WHILE STRUMMING ON HER GUITAR.

HOW GREAT THIS WILL BE, DAISY THOUGHT. I WILL NOW HAVE THE COMPANY OF A LOVING FAMILY, COMFORTABLE SURROUNDINGS, AND

GOOD FOOD. THE BONUS IS, I'LL ALSO HAVE A CHANCE TO MEET INTERESTING GUESTS FROM AROUND THE WORLD. THIS WAS BEYOND DAISY'S WILDEST EXPECTATION.

HER JOY WAS SHORT-LIVED. DAISY LEAPED OUT OF THE CAR WITH HER SUITCASE AND STARTED TO BOLT TOWARD THE HOUSE WHEN MR. RUFUS ARFED, "NO, DAISY! STAY! YOU WILL NOT BE LIVING IN THE INN. YOUR HOME IS THE BARN. YOU ARE HERE TO RID MY PROPERTY OF VERMIN. AFTER ALL, YOU ARE A RAT TERRIER."

"WHAT?" DAISY WHIMPERED. "I DON'T UNDERSTAND. I THOUGHT YOU WANTED ME TO HELP AT THE INN. YOU KNOW I HAVE MANY TALENTS. I SHOWED YOU THAT DURING MY PERFORMANCE AT THE OPEN HOUSE TONIGHT. I WILL WORK HARD FOR YOU INSIDE YOUR ESTABLISHMENT."

MR. RUFUS GLARED AT DAISY AND SHOOK HIS HEAD IN DISBELIEF. "YOU'LL GET YOUR WORK ORDERS FROM A MEMBER OF MY STAFF IN THE MORNING," HE GROWLED, AND HEADED FOR THE INN. "NOW GET IN THAT BARN WHERE YOU BELONG!"

DAISY STOOD ALONE IN THE DARK FOR A FEW MINUTES; FIRST HUMILIATED, THEN BARKING MAD. FOR AN INSTANT, SHE CONSIDERED RUNNING AWAY, BUT DAISY HAD MADE A COMMITMENT AND SHE WOULD STAND BY IT, AT LEAST FOR THE PRESENT.

DAISY ENTERED THE BARN AND SURVEYED HER BLEAK SURROUNDINGS. HER BED, TUCKED AWAY IN THE CORNER, WAS DILAPIDATED WITH BROKEN SPRINGS, AND THE MATTRESS WAS TERRIBLY WORN AND LUMPY. THE BLANKETS HAD NUMEROUS MOTH HOLES IN THEM, AND THERE WAS A BADLY STAINED AREA RUG FRONTING THE BED. A DIM LIGHT BULB WITH A PULL-STRING WAS HER ONLY SOURCE OF LIGHT. DOG-TIRED, BOTH EMOTIONALLY AND PHYSICALLY, SHE PLOPPED INTO BED, HOPING SHE WOULD BE BETTER ABLE TO COPE WITH THINGS THE NEXT DAY.

IN THE MORNING, DAISY WAS UP EARLY, SWEEPING COBWEBS FROM THE RAFTERS ABOVE HER BED, SEWING UP THE MOTH HOLES IN HER BLANKETS, AND SETTING UP A LIBRARY OF SOME OF HER FAVORITE NOVELS SHE BROUGHT ALONG, INCLUDING *FOR WHOM THE BALL ROLLS*,

THE OLD DOG AND THE FLEA, AND THE LOST DOG ALWAYS BARKS TWICE. A STAFF MEMBER FROM THE INN CAME BY WITH DAISY'S WORK ORDERS. SHE WAS TO PATROL A 50-ACRE EXTERIOR AREA WHICH COMPRISED THE INN, OUT-BUILDINGS, AND TEN COTTAGES. DAISY WAS NOT TO FRATERNIZE WITH GUESTS, AND TO BE AS UNOBTRUSIVE AS POSSIBLE AS SHE TENDED TO HER DUTY OF CHASING VERMIN OFF THE PREMISES. HER MEALS WOULD BE BROUGHT TO THE BARN AND WOULD CONSIST MOSTLY OF LEFTOVER SCRAPS.

MONTHS WENT BY, AND THE DAYS AND NIGHTS TURNED COLDER AS A BLANKET OF SNOW COVERED THE GROUND. WHILE DAISY SHIVERED IN THE BARN EVERY NIGHT, HER KEEN EARS PICKED UP THE SOUNDS OF GUESTS IN THE INN HAVING A GREAT TIME. IT WAS SAD TO REALIZE SHE WOULD NEVER BE INCLUDED, EVEN THOUGH SHE HAD EXCEEDED MR. RUFUS'S EXPECTATIONS; SCARING OFF TWICE AS MANY MICE AND RATS PER DAY AS HER PREDECESSOR, OLD HELLER. SHE ALSO MADE REPAIRS ON FENCES, CLEANED OUT BIRDHOUSES, AND TIDIED UP AROUND THE PONDS. DAISY EVEN HAD A LITTLE JESSICA FETCHER IN HER, AS SHE MADE NIGHTLY

INVESTIGATIONS TO ENSURE RACCOONS AND OTHER NOCTURNAL CREATURES WERE NOT CREATING HAVOC WITH THE GARBAGE CANS. BUT THERE WAS NEVER ACKNOWLEDGMENT OR APPRECIATION FROM MR. RUFUS FOR DAISY'S DEDICATION AND HARD WORK.

ONE NIGHT, AS DAISY SNIFFED THE AROMA OF BAKED BISCUIT—STUFFED CHICKEN FROM THE INN'S KITCHEN, AND SAW THE GUESTS, THROUGH THE PARLOR WINDOW, SEATED AROUND THE ROARING FIRE IN THE HEARTH ENGAGED IN LIVELY CONVERSATION, IT WAS TOO MUCH FOR HER TO BEAR. SHE RETURNED TO HER DREARY CORNER OF THE BARN AND BEGAN TO HOWL OUT A WOEFUL BLUES TUNE, *THIS HOUND'S SO LONESOME SHE COULD CRY.*

THE GUESTS IN THE INN STOPPED THEIR CONVERSATIONS IN MID—YAP AND PERKED UP THEIR EARS TO LISTEN. CODY, A ROUGH COLLIE, WAS THE FIRST TO BARK UP: "WHO IS SINGING? THAT IS ONE OF THE MOST REMARKABLE VOICES I HAVE EVER HEARD."

"IT'S JUST THE RATTER IN THE BARN," MR. RUFUS GROWLED. "I'LL SEND MY DOG—SERVANT OUT TO SHUT 'ER UP."

CODY SAT UP AND BARKED, "DOGONNIT, RUFUS, WHAT KIND OF BITING COMMENT IS THAT? THAT POOR SOUL IS OBVIOUSLY HURTING. WHERE IS YOUR COMPASSION?" CODY STORMED OUT THE DOOR AND TROTTED OVER TO THE BARN.

"WE NEED TO TALK," CODY GENTLY BARKED, AFTER INTRODUCING HIMSELF TO DAISY. CODY WAS A WELL-CONNECTED TALENT SCOUT FOR THE MUSIC INDUSTRY. HE WANTED TO KNOW ALL ABOUT DAISY'S LIFE AND SHOWED A WARMTH AND KINDNESS THAT ALLOWED DAISY TO RELATE HER SAD STORY TO HIM.

CODY CONFIDENTLY WOOFED, "I WANT TO TAKE YOU TO A PLACE WHERE YOU WILL BE APPRECIATED, AND YOUR TALENT WILL TOUCH THE HEARTS OF MANY CANINES...ALL THE WAY TO THE TOP: HOLLYWOOD, CALIFORNIA. I CAN MAKE YOU A STAR."

"BUT LOOK AT ME," DAISY WHIMPERED. "THEY WOULD HOWL AT ME. I AM NOT ONE OF THE BEAUTIFUL POOCHES."

"AH, BUT THAT IS WHERE YOU ARE WRONG," CODY YELPED. "TALENT TRUMPS LOOKS, AND

YOUR STORY WILL INSPIRE OTHERS. JUST LOOK AT THAT KINDLY OLD ENGLISH BULLDOG, SUSAN BOYLEHOUND, ON BRITAIN'S BARKIN' UP TALENT."

THERE WAS NO OTHER ANSWER FOR HER BUT "YES," AND DAISY WENT WITH CODY TO TELL MR. RUFUS SHE WANTED TO LEAVE.

"WHAT?" RUFUS SHOWED HIS TEETH, "I PAID PLENTY FOR YOU."

CODY CASUALLY TOOK OUT HIS POOCH BAG AND SETTLED THAT ISSUE WITH 500 GREENBARKS AND A GOLD-ENCRUSTED BISCUIT COIN.

CODY AND DAISY PROMPTLY LEFT TO BEGIN WORKING ON HER NEW CAREER. DAISY'S FASCINATION WITH REALITY TV LED CODY TO YIP, "ARE YOU UP TO TRYING OUT FOR *AMERICAN HOWLER?*"

DAISY'S EARS PITCHED FORWARD WITH KEEN INTEREST, AND SHE BARKED, "LET'S GO FOR IT!"

Leg II
Daisy Goes Hollywood

Rodeo Drive Shopper

WHILE PACKING HER LUGGAGE, DAISY REALIZED SHE NEEDED TO REVAMP HER WARDROBE; HER COUNTRY CLOTHES WERE SIMPLY NOT APPROPRIATE. SHE WENT TO A LOCAL CATSIGNMENT SHOP WHERE SHE FOUND AN OUTFIT SHE WAS ABLE TO ALTER INTO A RETRO-LOOKING COSTUME. IT WAS PERFECT FOR MIAMI, FLORIDA WHERE THE *AMERICAN HOWLER* REGIONAL AUDITIONS WERE HELD. DAISY WAS ONE OF THOSE MULTITALENTED DOGS WHO COULD SING, DANCE, PAINT, COOK, AND DESIGN HER OWN CLOTHING. SHE WAS LOOKING FORWARD TO UNLEASHING ALL THAT LATENT CREATIVITY AND SEEING WHERE IT COULD TAKE HER.

SEVERAL DAYS LATER, DAISY WAS BOARDING A PLANE TO THE SUNSHINE STATE. SHE HAD ONE QUICK STOP TO MAKE UPON ARRIVAL: THE TATTOO PARLOR OF RENOWNED BODY ARTIST, MIAMI PINK, A SASSY PINK TOY POODLE WHOSE LIMBS WERE HEAVILY ADORNED WITH HER CRAFT. DAISY ASKED MIAMI TO ENHANCE HER BIRTHMARK — INSTEAD OF LOOKING LIKE AN ACCIDENT OF NATURE, IT'D BE AN ARTISTIC STATEMENT. THE RAGGED DAISY IMAGE WAS BEAUTIFIED WITH INTRICATE COLOR LINE

WORK — THEN A SMALL DIAMOND, RESEMBLING
A GLISTENING DEWDROP, WAS STRATEGICALLY
PLACED ON ONE OF THE PETALS.

Miami Pink

THE NEXT DAY, DAISY STOOD IN THE LONG LINE IN FRONT OF THE *AMERICAN HOWLER* STUDIO, NERVOUSLY AWAITING HER SINGING DEBUT. HER AGENT, CODY, HAD ADVISED HER TO KEEP HER YAPPING UNDER CONTROL WHILE INTRODUCING HERSELF TO THE JUDGES. SHE NEEDED TO PROJECT A CALM DEMEANOR AND NOT BE ANNOYING. SOME OF THE CANINES WERE ACTING SILLY, PRATTLING AND CLOWNING AROUND IN OUTLANDISH COSTUMES. WHEN THEY WERE NOT CHOSEN, THEY DISPLAYED REALLY BAD BEHAVIOR, BARING TEETH, JUMPING UP AND DOWN ON THE COUCHES, AND GROWLING ABOUT HOW SHABBILY THEY HAD BEEN TREATED.

WHEN THE HOST OF *AMERICAN HOWLER*, RYAN SEADOG, CALLED DAISY'S NAME, SHE TOOK HER ENTRY FORM FROM HIM AND ENTERED THE ROOM WHERE THE FOUR JUDGES WERE SEATED. THE PANEL CONSISTED OF AN ENGLISH FOXHOUND, BLACK LABRADOR RETRIEVER, CAIRN TERRIER, AND A COCKER SPANIEL. DAISY WALKED, WITH APPREHENSION, IN FRONT OF THE JUDGES AND ENGAGED IN SOME SMALL BARK UNTIL SHE WAS ASKED TO PERFORM. SHE LET LOOSE A ROUSING A CAPPELLA RENDITION

OF *HOWLING MY HEART OUT OVER YOU* — THEN WAITED FOR THE JUDGES' REACTIONS. THREE JUDGES RESPONDED FAVORABLY, BUT THE ENGLISH FOXHOUND, SIMON HOWL, WHO HAD BEEN RUDELY YAWNING AND STRETCHING THROUGHOUT DAISY'S ENTIRE AUDITION, BARKED, "I ALMOST ROLLED OVER AND PLAYED DEAD DURING THAT GHASTLY PERFORMANCE."

HIS COMMENTS WERE MET WITH AN ANGRY CHORUS OF GROWLS AND CATCALLS FROM THE OTHER JUDGES AND STUDIO PRODUCTION CREW. DAISY JUST STOOD THERE, LOOKING STRAIGHT AHEAD WITH SAD PUPPY EYES. DESPITE THOSE HURTFUL WORDS, DAISY WAS THRILLED TO HEAR POSITIVE COMMENTS FROM THE OTHER JUDGES. THE GUEST JUDGE, STEVEN TERRIER, WITH HIS WILD UNKEMPT HAIR AND MULTIPLE CHAINS AROUND HIS NECK, WAS ESPECIALLY ATTENTIVE, STARING AT DAISY AND ARFING, "LIKED IT, DOLL. HAS ANYONE TOLD YOU YOU'RE A REAL CUTIE?" WITH THREE OF THE FOUR JUDGES RAISING THEIR PAWS, THE BLACK LAB ENTHUSIASTICALLY PROCLAIMED, "DAISY, YOU ARE THE BOMB. YOU'RE GOING TO HOLLYWOOD, DAWG!"

DAISY ARRIVED IN TINSELTOWN AND MOVED INTO A MANSION WITH OTHER FIRST-LEVEL CONTESTANTS. THE WINNER OF *AMERICAN HOWLER* WAS SLATED TO RECEIVE A RECORDING CONTRACT, PLUS AN INVITATION TO PARTICIPATE IN ANOTHER PRESTIGIOUS CONTEST, *THE WORLD'S MOST SPECTACULAR DOG* COMPETITION, A REALITY SHOW TRIATHLON COMBINING THREE OTHER HIGH-PROFILE REALITY PROGRAMS.

EACH WEEK, THE *AMERICAN HOWLER* COMPETITION BECAME TOUGHER AND TOUGHER. CONTESTANTS WERE REQUIRED TO HOWL ALONG TO DIFFERENT GENRES OF MUSIC. FAMOUS ARTISTS WOULD COME BY THE STUDIOS AND HELP THE CONTESTANTS PRACTICE AND STRENGTHEN THEIR VOCALS. DAISY WAS ECSTATIC WHEN THREE OF HER FAVORITE RECORDING ARTISTS VISITED: THE ARTIST FORMERLY KNOWN AS SPOT, A DALMATIAN; MADDOGA, THE ENGLISH SPRINGER SPANIEL; AND THE OUTRAGEOUSLY COIFFED POMERANIAN, LADY PAW PAW. WHEN HIP-HOP ARTISTS CURIOUS DOG, A GERMAN SHEPHERD, MINIATURE DACHSHUND LIL' HOUND, AND THE ROTTWEILER, 2 CENT, CAME BY, ALL THREE HOWLED WITH APPRECIATIVE LAUGHTER

WHEN DAISY PRESENTED HER OWN ORIGINAL COMPOSITION:

"PAWS ARE TAPPIN'

FRIENDS ARE RAPPIN'

WHIPS IN THE HOOD

PLAYIN' EMCEES GOOD

SHORTY'S WEARIN' BLING, GRILL, AND ICE

HE SAYS, 'HOLLA! BE FLOSSEN: THOSE

CATS ARE BALIN' NICE.'"

FOLLOWING HER PERFORMANCE, DAISY WAS MADE AN HONORARY MEMBER OF THE HIP-HOP COMMUNITY, AND THE BOYZ ANOINTED HER "CHOCOLATE CHIP".

AMERICAN HOWLER WAS A SENSATIONAL EXPERIENCE FOR DAISY AND, FOR THE FIRST TIME IN HER LIFE, SHE WAS APPRECIATED. WHEN SHE GOT TO THE FINAL FIVE AND LOOKED OUT OVER THE THOUSANDS OF SCREAMING FANS IN THE AUDITORIUM, SHE REALIZED WHAT HER FRIENDS HAD BEEN TELLING HER WHEN LIFE WAS SO TOUGH: IN THE END, HER TALENT WOULD SET HER APART. SHE REMEMBERED HOW

SHE FELT WHEN THINGS SEEMED SO HOPELESS JUST A SHORT TIME AGO. SHE CERTAINLY COULD RELATE TO AFFENPINSCHER RODNEY DOGGERFIELD'S PET PHRASE, "I DON'T GET NO RESPECT." BUT NOW SHE HAD IT IN SPADES.

DAISY BASKED IN THE LIMELIGHT AS THE COMPETITION RACED TO ITS CONCLUSION. SHE WAS GIVEN AN *AMERICAN HOWLER* PARADE IN HER SMALL PENNSYLVANIA HOMETOWN AFTER SHE MADE IT INTO THE FINALS. DAISY WAS SURPRISED TO SEE A HUGE NUMBER OF DOGS AND CATS LINING MAIN STREET TO WAVE AT HER — OR GET CLOSE ENOUGH TO PET HER. EVEN SOME OF THOSE WHO HAD NOT BEEN KIND TO HER WERE IN ATTENDANCE. RIDING ALONGSIDE HER IN THE CAR WERE CODY AND, OF COURSE, WOOLLY. DAISY NEVER FORGOT THOSE WHO WERE THERE FOR HER IN THE BEGINNING.

DAISY GOT ALONG WITH MOST OF THE FINAL CONTESTANTS EXCEPT FOR THE PEKINGESE, JADE, WHO HAD A SNIPPY, CONDESCENDING ATTITUDE. JADE CAME FROM A SMALL MIDWESTERN TOWN AND ASPIRED TO BREAK INTO SHOW BUSINESS. SHE MOVED TO NEW

YORK CITY AND WAITED TABLES NIGHTLY AT THE HOWLING NOTE COFFEEHOUSE, WHILE GOING ON CATTLE CALLS DURING THE DAY. SHE JUMPED FOR JOY WHEN AN OLD DOG WITH HOLLYWOOD CONNECTIONS, WHO LOVED HER FRISKY DEMEANOR, ARRANGED FOR HER TO PARTICIPATE IN THE REALITY TALENT SHOW AFTER HEARING HER SING DURING OPEN MIKE NIGHT AT THE COFFEEHOUSE. JADE THOUGHT HER SINGING TALENT WAS BETTER THAN IT ACTUALLY WAS. SHE BOASTED TO THE OTHER CANINES THAT SHE WAS THE ONLY FINALIST WHO WAS CLASSICALLY TRAINED.

IN FACT, JADE WAS NEVER ACCEPTED AT BULLIARD; SHE'D ONLY TAKEN A ONE-MONTH COURSE AT MAZIE & FIDO'S MUSIC SCHOOL IN THE BRONX.

THE TIME HAD COME TO DETERMINE WHO WOULD BE NAMED THE WINNER OF *AMERICAN HOWLER*. EACH OF THE FIVE REMAINING CANINES WAS ASSIGNED A SONG TO PERFORM DURING THE FINAL TV EPISODE. AN INTERNATIONAL AUDIENCE WOULD BE CHOOSING THE WINNER BY TEXTING IN THEIR VOTES.

THE SONGS MATCHED THE CONTESTANTS PERFECTLY:

BERNARD, THE BASSET HOUND, WAS GIVEN *FOG HORNS IN THE NIGHT*;

THE BASENJI, BOBBIE SUE, WOULD SING *SQUIRREL HOLLOW SQUALOR*;

TUNE, THE NEW GUINEA SINGING DOG, HAD A HIP-HOP SELECTION, *HOOD HAPPENINGS AT MY CRIB*;

THE PEKINGESE, JADE, WAS TO PERFORM A SULTRY INTERPRETATION OF *A TIME FOR PROWLING AND GROWLING*;

AND DAISY WAS ASSIGNED *TERRIERS JUST LOVE TO DIG*.

BERNARD HAD A "REBEL LOOK" ABOUT HIM WITH HIS ABUNDANT JOWLS, LONG EARS, AND SANDPAPER BEARD. HIS SIMPLE ATTIRE CONSISTED OF FADED JEANS, A FITTED, BUTTON-DOWN WHITE SHIRT, AND WOODEN BEADS. BUT BERNARD WAS IMPRESSIVE ON STAGE AS HE PLAYED HIS TUBA DURING PART OF HIS PERFORMANCE, GIVING HIS SELECTION A MUSICAL INTERPRETATION OF

A FOG HORN. IT WAS THE PERFECT PAIRING TO HIS DEEP, MUSICAL BARK.

BOBBIE SUE, A COUNTRY MUSIC SINGER-SONGWRITER, HAD DEVELOPED HER TALENT IN HER NATIVE CLARKSDALE, MISSISSIPPI WHERE SHE'D GONE TO JUKE JOINTS TO LISTEN TO ARTISTS HOWLIN' DOG, LICK TURNER, B.B. FANG, AND MUDDY BARKERS. BOBBIE SUE LOOKED LIKE THE ULTIMATE COUNTRY PERFORMER ON THE *AMERICAN HOWLER* STAGE WITH HER BIG HAIR, OFF-THE-SHOULDER RUFFLED DRESS, AND TURQUOISE-ENCRUSTED COWBOY BOOTS. SHE DELIGHTED THE AUDIENCE WITH HER FUN, GIGGLY PERSONALITY AND YODEL-BARK SINGING STYLE.

WHEN TUNE GRABBED THE MICROPHONE, HE ELECTRIFIED THE CROWD WITH HIS FIRST NOTE...A WOLF-LIKE HIGH HOWL. HE WAS A RARE BREED TO BE SURE, DECKED OUT IN HIS SIGNATURE URBAN STYLE DOUBLE-BREASTED SUIT JACKET, ALLIGATOR-SKIN SHOES, OVERSIZED SUNGLASSES, AND DO-RAG. TUNE HAD THE ABILITY TO DRAMATICALLY CHANGE THE PITCH OF HIS VOCALS WHILE

YAPPING HIS RAP SONGS, AND HIS TALENT AS A SMOOTH BREAK DANCER MADE HIM ONE OF THE FRONT-RUNNERS OF THE COMPETITION.

IT WAS A JAW-DROPPING MOMENT FOR THE OTHER FOUR CONTESTANTS WHEN JADE FIRST APPEARED ON STAGE FROM BEHIND THE CURTAIN. SHE WAS GLAMOUR PERSONIFIED, WEARING A FLIRTY JADE GREEN SEQUIN MINI DRESS WITH MATCHING LACED LIMO HEELS, DIAMOND CHANDELIER EARRINGS, AND A CHUNKY DIAMOND CUFF BRACELET. HER POUTY MOUTH WAS ENHANCED WITH A SHOT OF COLLAGEN. THE STYLIST, RACHEL DOE, HAD BEEN INVOLVED IN THIS REMARKABLE TRANSFORMATION. JADE WHIPPED UP THE MALE DOGS IN THE AUDIENCE INTO SUCH A FRENZY THAT SHE HAD TO SHRILLY BARK OUT HER SONG OVER THEIR MANIACAL BAYING. IT WAS SO BAD SIMON HOWL WHISPERED SARCASTICALLY TO THE OTHER JUDGES, "EGAD, THAT ALMOST RUPTURED MY EARDRUM. WHERE DID SHE SAY SHE SANG? THE HOWLING NOTE? IT SHOULD BE CALLED THE DYING NOTE!"

DAISY GOT SET TO FOLLOW JADE'S

SPECTACULAR APPEARANCE. SHE GLANCED DOWN AT HERSELF AND THOUGHT, HOW CAN I EVER COMPETE WITH JADE? I'M WEARING HUMBLE PAW-SEWN CLOTHING I DESIGNED MYSELF, AND HAVE CHEAP COSTUME JEWELRY. IT DID NOT OCCUR TO DAISY THAT HER SUPERIOR TALENT WOULD MEAN MUCH MORE TO THOSE WATCHING THE COMPETITION THAN EYE CANDY.

DAISY'S LIFE STORY WAS NOW WELL KNOWN, AND SHE HAD MANY FANS GLOBALLY. SHE WALKED IN FRONT OF THE JUDGES AND THE AUDIENCE, AND WAS ENCOURAGED BY THE ENTHUSIASTIC AND RESPECTFUL WELCOME SHE GOT FROM THE CROWD. SHE HAD HER GUITAR WITH HER FOR THIS SONG, A COMBINATION OF BLUES AND POP MUSIC. DAISY SAT ON A STOOL AND BEGAN STRUMMING A SOFT INTRODUCTION. SHE JOINED THE INSTRUMENTAL MELODY, SINGING WITH SUCH PERFECTION AND EMOTION THAT IT BROUGHT TEARS TO THE EYES OF MANY IN THE AUDIENCE. SINGING A CAPPELLA, WHEN SHE HIT THE FINAL HIGH NOTE, THE ROOM WENT WILD.

Daisy Howling Her Song

NEVER BEFORE HAD DAISY FELT SO HONORED AS WHEN THE CROWD GAVE HER A SITTING OVATION. DAISY WON THE *AMERICAN HOWLER* COMPETITION PAWS-DOWN.

ALONG WITH HER HOWLER VICTORY CAME ACCESS TO VIDs (VERY IMPORTANT DOGS). DAISY RECEIVED INVITATIONS TO MANY PRESTIGIOUS SOCIAL EVENTS — EVERYTHING FROM BEACH PARTIES IN MALIBU TO RED CARPET GALAS. EVERY DOG WANTED TO BE HER BEST FRIEND. IT WAS A MOMENTOUS TIME FOR DAISY — ONCE A HOMELESS COUNTRY DOG, SHE WAS SUDDENLY THE TOAST OF THE TOWN.

She attended soirees in Los Angeles and watched dapper movie-mogul Shar Peis working the room with elegant Shih Tzus, Miniature Poodles, and Yorkshire Terriers, decked out in diamond-studded collars and near-endangered species furs. A few cougars were in attendance too.

Air-kissing, paw bumps, slobbering, and tongue-wagging were common sights. Only the privileged were there...the "top dogs"... and Daisy got a first-paw education on all types of upper-canine social behavior.

Daisy chuckled when she spotted two party-crashing Salukis sneaking into the private California-style luau she attended on Billionaire's Beach in Malibu. They had gotten past Bo, the Saint Bernard bouncer, who was obviously sleeping on the job (or nipping from the whiskey barrel). There they go again, thought Daisy, as she watched this blatant intrusion. The two made a B-line to entertainment interviewers Bone Slivers and her daughter, Biscuit, Smooth Fox Terriers who were standing at the gate on the painted red sand, waiting

TO POUNCE ON THEIR NEXT INTERVIEW. THE SALUKIS WERE HAPPY TO OBLIGE, THIRSTING TO GET 15 MORE MINUTES OF FAME.

TRAYS OF APPETIZERS...DUCK LIVER PATE, TURKEY JERKY, LOBSTER RABBIT RAREBIT SNAPS, BACON PUDDING BITES, AND DIFFERENT TYPES OF LIBATION WERE PASSED AROUND BY STRAY FELINE WAITRESSES WHO HAD PREVIOUSLY WORKED A BRUNCH AT NEARBY KIBBLE BEACH GOLF CLUB.

SOME HIGH-MAINTENANCE SOCIALITE GUESTS, LIKE COUNTESS VIVIENNE BARKER-BAYED, A BICHON FRISE WHO WAS WEARING A BEAUTIFUL DIAMOND TIARA, BROUGHT THEIR ENTIRE ENTOURAGES OF FUR AND TOENAIL STYLISTS WITH THEM TO THE PARTY.

Malibu Sun Worshipper

WHEN DAISY HAD SEEN ENOUGH AND DECIDED TO DEPART, ON HER WAY OUT THE GATE SHE WAS TREATED TO A DOGGIE GOODIE BAG FILLED WITH CERTIFICATES FOR PRETTY CLAWS PETICURE SALON, BESS'S TRESSES, ARFER'S BAKERY, BAMBI'S NIP AND TUCK CLINIC, AND A PRIVATE JEWELRY SHOWING AT HAIRY LISSOME, THE LEGENDARY STORE OWNED BY THAT DISTINCTIVE GREYHOUND WITH A GREAT TRACK RECORD. DAISY GRABBED HER BAG AND THOUGHT, *HMMM...IT'S SO COOL BEING AN A-LISTER!*

DAISY ACCEPTED A FEW PROMOTIONAL GIGS HERE AND THERE IN ADDITION TO WORKING ON HER RECORDING DEAL WITH *AMERICAN HOWLER.* ONE NIGHT SHE WAS A GUEST WRESTLER AT THE *WWWOOF* AND TOOK ON THE POWERFULLY BUILT AMERICAN MASTIFF, BULK DOGAN. WHEN SHE STEPPED INTO THE RING, SHE LOOKED EVERY BIT THE DIVA WITH HER RHINESTONE COSTUME AND MATCHING CAPE — ONE OF HER DESIGNS FROM HER NEW CLOTHING LINE, DAISY'S DUDS. NIPPING AT BULK'S ANKLES, SPINNING AROUND, AND YAPPING WILDLY WAS ENOUGH TO EXHAUST THE BIG WRESTLER, AND HE WAS SOON DOWN FOR

THE COUNT. BUT SOME TV CRITICS FELT THE MATCH, LIKE BULK HIMSELF, MIGHT HAVE BEEN FIXED.

CALIFORNIA WAS A GREAT PLACE TO OWN A MOTORCYCLE. DAISY JOINED A BIKER CLUB, HOUNDS ON HOGS, AND WOULD RIDE HER HARLEY HIGH ABOVE THE PACIFIC OCEAN ON HIGHWAY 1. DAISY'S CYCLE STOOD OUT WITH HER DISTINCTIVE BUMPER STICKER: "I BRAKE FOR, AND BARK AT, SQUIRRELS!" SHE FELT A SENSE OF FREEDOM AS SHE SPED ALONG WITH THIS PACK OF ADVENTUROUS BEAGLES IN HER LEATHER BIKER GARB, FEELING THE WIND IN HER FUR, AND HAVING THAT SENSE OF CAMARADERIE WITH HER NEW FRIENDS.

DAISY ALSO CULTIVATED FRIENDSHIPS WITH SOME OF THE HOLLYWOOD STARS AND SOUGHT OUT THEIR ADVICE. SHE WANTED TO LEARN AS MUCH AS POSSIBLE ABOUT THE CULTURE AND TRADITIONS OF THIS FASCINATING COMMUNITY. IT WASN'T UNUSUAL TO SEE DAISY YAPPING WITH DAWG THE BOUNTY HUNTER, A BLOODHOUND WHO'D OFTEN INVITE DAISY TO A NEIGHBORHOOD STAKE-OUT. SHE GOT ASSERTIVENESS TRAINING FROM DOOZY O'DOGGELL, A PUG WITH VERY

STRONG OPINIONS WHO KNEW HOW TO GET WHAT SHE WANTED; AND VOICE COACHING FROM AIREDALE TERRIER AND TV ANCHOR, LOU DOGGS. FELINE PROTOCOL EXPERT, THE VERY PROPER MISS KATRINA, COACHED DAISY ON ETIQUETTE AND CUSTOMS OF PEOPLE FROM DIFFERENT COUNTRIES AROUND THE WORLD WHOM SHE WOULD BE MEETING. SHE ALSO TAUGHT HER SPANISH, AND DAISY COULD NOW PROUDLY BARK, "I'M BOWLINGUAL."

Miss Katrina, Daisy's Protocol Coach

THE HOLLYWOOD LIFE WAS GOOD...A LITTLE TOO GOOD...AND UNFORTUNATELY THE LIFESTYLE SOON OVERTOOK DAISY. SHE WAS STAYING OUT LATE EVERY NIGHT WITH ONE-NAME PARTY ANIMALS, RARIST, BRATNEY, AND DITZY AT THE BOW-WOW CLUB ON THE SUNSET STRIP; DANCING SALSA WITH CHIHUAHUA MARIO POOCHEZ IN LATIN CLUBS...THEN GETTING UP LATE IN THE MORNING TO SHOP THE EXCLUSIVE BEVERLY HILLS BOUTIQUE STORES LIKE BARKEY'S, DOG SACS, AND CATIER. LONG LUNCHES USUALLY FOLLOWED AT THE IVY OR MR. CHOW'S ROADHOUSE. DAISY HAD RAPIDLY "GONE HOLLYWOOD" AND WAS FREQUENTLY SEEN STRUTTING DOWN RODEO DRIVE WEARING HER LARGE PRADA CAT'S EYE SUNGLASSES, AND TOTING NUMEROUS SHOPPING BAGS. SHE WAS EASY GAME FOR THE PUPARAZZI AND MEDIA HOUNDS WHO FOUND EVERY OPPORTUNITY TO PHOTOGRAPH AND INTERVIEW HER FOR THE TABLOIDS.

DAISY ALSO KEPT AN EXHAUSTING SCHEDULE AS A REGULAR ON THE BARK SHOW CIRCUIT, FREQUENTING THE GUEST COUCHES OF OPURR, CHELSEA DOGHANDLER, JIMMY KIBBLE, JAYBIRD LENO AND DAVID LITTERMAN. IN

HER LATER YEARS SHE JOINED THE HENS ON *THE SQUAWK*, BRINGING ALONG SOME OF HER FELINE AND CANINE FRIENDS TO HISS AND GROWL IN THE STUDIO AUDIENCE; AND ALSO ACCEPTED A STARRING ROLE ON THE DAYTIME DRAMA SHOW, *THE OLD AND THE LISTLESS.*

Opurr
Bark Show Host Extraordinaire

FAME WAS HAPPENING TOO FAST. CONCERNED FRIENDS FREQUENTLY NOTICED DAISY POSING WITH A FAKE SMILE, HOPING TO BE PHOTOGRAPHED, A LITTLE TOO MUCH. IF THAT DID NOT HAPPEN, SHE'D PULL OUT HER SELFIE STICK AND SEND HER OWN PICTURES TO THE MEDIA. SHE WAS CONSTANTLY SHOUTING OUT HER INFORMATION ON YIP YAP AS WELL. SHE

WAS SPOTTED HANGING AROUND NEWSSTANDS LATE AT NIGHT, WAITING FOR THE TRADE MAGAZINES TO ARRIVE SO SHE COULD READ ABOUT HERSELF IN *DOG VARIETIES* AND *THE HOLLYWOOD RETRIEVER*. BUT LIKE MOST CELEBRITIES, DAISY HATED THE TABLOIDS. WHEN DISTURBING GOSSIP APPEARED ABOUT HER IN *THE TALL-TAIL ENQUIRER*, DAISY WOULD BUY UP ALL THE COPIES AND TEAR THEM TO SHREDS IN THE ALLEYS BEHIND THE NEWSSTANDS.

IT WAS TIME, WOOLLY AND SEVERAL OF DAISY'S OTHER FRIENDS DECIDED, TO HOLD AN INTERVENTION. DAISY HAD TO AGREE SHE DID NOT LIKE WHAT SHE WAS BECOMING, AND CONSENTED TO SEEK THE COUNSEL OF THE GREAT DANE, DR. PHIL McGROWL. MONTHS OF EXTENSIVE THERAPY HELPED DAISY TO SEE HOW HER DESTRUCTIVE BEHAVIOR WAS UNDERMINING THE CORE VALUES SHE HELD SO DEAR. WITH DR. McGROWL'S COUNSELING, DAISY WAS ABLE TO BOUNCE BACK, REGAIN HER HUMILITY, AND BECOME MORE CONFIDENT AND STRONGER THAN EVER AS SHE BEGAN PREPARING FOR *THE WORLD'S MOST SPECTACULAR DOG* COMPETITION.

ONE DAY, DAISY RECEIVED A PHONE CALL FROM A HOLLYWOOD FILMMAKER WHO GOT HER PANTING WITH EXCITEMENT. HE WANTED TO MEET DAISY FOR DINNER AND, AS HE PUT IT, "DISCUSS YOUR MOVIE CAREER."

THIS COULD BE MY BIG BREAK, DAISY THOUGHT. *COULD THINGS GET ANY BETTER?*

IT SEEMED THE ROUGH TIMES WERE FINALLY BEHIND DAISY...OR WERE THEY?

Leg III
The Dognapping

Filmmaker Michael "Puggy" Pugnose

THE EXCITED CANINE HAD TO RESTRAIN HERSELF FROM RUNNING AROUND IN CIRCLES AS SHE WAITED AT THE ENTRANCE OF SPAGO BEVERLY HILLS FOR HER HOST. SHE FINALLY SPOTTED THE CORPULENT CUR WADDLING UP THE STAIRS, BREATHING HEAVILY WITH SWEAT POURING FROM HIS WRINKLED BROW. MICHAEL PUGNOSE (AKA "PUGGY"), A BOXER,

WORE A POORLY-FITTED BLUE SUIT WITH A LOOSENED TIE, A RUMPLED BASEBALL CAP, AND ROUND WIRE EYEGLASSES. HE HAD A CIGAR CLENCHED IN HIS TEETH AND, AS HE APPROACHED DAISY WITH HIS DISTINCTIVE SWAGGER, PUGGY INTRODUCED HIMSELF WITH A LOW, THROATY GROWL.

THEY WERE SEATED AND PUGGY'S DIALOGUE STARTED OUT CORDIAL, BUT IT RAPIDLY CHANGED TO OBSESSIVE AND UNPLEASANT GROWLING ABOUT PROMOTING HIS NEWEST TALENT AND LOVE INTEREST, JADE, THE PEKINGESE WHO WAS DAISY'S TOUGHEST RIVAL DURING THE *AMERICAN HOWLER* COMPETITION.

HOLY HOTDOG, DAISY THOUGHT, AS HER EARS ANGLED BACK, *THIS DUDE HAS SOME SERIOUS AGGRESSION ISSUES. HE IS DEFINITELY MARKING HIS TERRITORY.*

PUGGY BARKED, "I'VE BEEN FOLLOWING THE NEWS OF HOW YOU'VE BEEN A BAD DOG."

OH-OH, DAISY THOUGHT. *IS HE TRYING TO PULL MY CHAIN?*

THE FILMMAKER KNEW DAISY WAS VULNERABLE, AND HE PLANNED TO USE THIS TO HIS ADVANTAGE. JADE WOULD ALSO BE A CONTESTANT IN THE UPCOMING *WORLD'S MOST SPECTACULAR DOG* COMPETITION AND DAISY WAS A THREAT TO HIS SWEETIE WINNING THE CROWN. IN ADDITION, PUGGY HAD INSIDE INFORMATION THAT DAISY WAS BEING CONSIDERED FOR THE STARRING ROLE IN THE WANNABE MOVIE, *TAME*, WHICH JADE WANTED BADLY.

THE AGITATED BOXER BIT INTO DAISY: "YOU DON'T HAVE WHAT IT TAKES TO BE A BIG STAR. YOU'RE NOTHIN' BUT A HOUND DOG, A COUNTRY BUMPKIN, A LOSER. EVERYONE IN HOLLYWOOD IS LAUGHING AT YOU BEHIND YOUR BACK. YOU DON'T BELONG HERE, DOG-EAR! I'M GIVING YOU ONE CHANCE TO GET OUTTA TOWN!"

DAISY PUSHED HERSELF AWAY FROM THE TABLE AND BARKED LOUDLY, "NO! I WILL NOT GIVE UP MY DREAM!" SHE BOLTED OUT THE RESTAURANT AND THROUGH THE DARK PARKING LOT, SOBBING UNCONTROLLABLY.

DAISY DIDN'T NOTICE THE SLEEK BLACK LIMO PULLING UP BESIDE HER. TWO DOBERMANS JUMPED OUT OF THE CAR, GRABBED HER, AND FORCED HER INTO THE BACK SEAT WITH THEM. PUGGY HOPPED INTO THE FRONT PASSENGER SEAT AND THEY SPED AWAY.

DAISY WAS SHAKEN AND BEWILDERED. SHE THOUGHT, *WHAT HAVE I DONE TO MAKE THIS CRAZY CUR WANT TO GET RID OF ME?*

SOON THEY WERE HIGH UP ON MULHOLLAND DRIVE. IT WAS LATE AT NIGHT, AND THERE WERE NO OTHER CARS ON THE WINDING DARK ROAD. BELOW, TO THE RIGHT, WAS A VIEW OF THE SAN FERNANDO VALLEY WITH TWINKLING LIGHTS SPREAD OUT AS FAR AS THE EYE COULD SEE, AND ACROSS THE ROAD WERE MANSIONS NESTLED IN THE HILLS ABOVE.

THE LIMOUSINE STOPPED ALONG THE SIDE OF THE ROAD JUST ABOVE THE HOLLYWOOD SIGN. DAISY WAS YANKED FROM THE CAR BY THE TWO BODYGUARDS AND HELD IN FRONT OF THEIR BOSS.

"OK," barked Puggy, "So you wanna play hardball? You had your chance. You shoulda listened to me!"

The Doberman muscle doghandled her down to the sign, commanded her, "Sit!" and tied her front paws to the base of the giant letter "D". The limo sped away, leaving Daisy shivering like a bunny. Her tiny form could not have been seen from below, and the road above was much too high up for her to be spotted by a passing motorist. She remembered some advice given to her by Dr. McGrowl: "Draw on your gifts, your resources, to get you out of trouble, should any come your way."

Daisy remembered that when she sewed her outfits, she always used her razor-sharp teeth instead of a scissors. She began to frantically gnaw away at the ropes that bound her limbs to the Hollywood sign. But the Dobermans were clever. They had coiled wire around the ropes, making it impossible for Daisy to chew herself free. Her mind raced, trying

TO FIND A WAY OUT OF HER DILEMMA WHEN SHE SPOTTED SOMETHING INCHING TOWARD HER FROM THE PITCH BLACK WOODED AREA. THEN SHE HEARD IT — THE EERIE, MOURNFUL HOWL OF A COYOTE, A SOUND SHE REMEMBERED FROM HER PUPPY FARM DAYS IN PENNSYLVANIA. SHE HAD ALWAYS BEEN FEARFUL OF COYOTES, AND FOR GOOD REASON: SMALL DOGS LIKE HER WERE ATTRACTIVE PREY FOR THESE CUNNING AND VICIOUS ANIMALS.

TO HER HORROR, DAISY SAW NOT ONE, BUT FIVE COYOTES STALKING HER. THEIR PIERCING EYES WERE FOCUSED ON HER MENACINGLY. THE LIGHT FROM THE FULL MOON BOUNCED OFF THEM, CASTING A SURREAL YELLOW-ORANGE GLOW.

DAISY THOUGHT SHE WAS A DOGGONER UNTIL THE ALPHA COYOTE DECIDED TO SHOW OFF FOR HIS PACK AND BAYED AT THE MOON. DAISY RECOGNIZED THE NOTE AND BAYED SKYWARD ONE NOTE HIGHER WITH PERFECT PITCH. THE COYOTE ACCEPTED THE CHALLENGE AND TOPPED HER NOTE. DAISY TOOK A DEEP BREATH AND HIT A HIGH-C FALSETTO THAT SHOOK THE SIGN. WHEN THE ALPHA COYOTE

TRIED TO MATCH IT, HIS VOICE BROKE OFF IN A HACKING COUGH. HE DARTED OFF INTO THE WOODS IN EMBARRASSMENT, FOLLOWED BY HIS DISAPPOINTED PACK.

DAISY REALIZED THAT HER STELLAR VOICE WAS HER TICKET TO FREEDOM. SHE BEGAN TO HOWL OUT AN S–O–S THAT REVERBERATED INTO THE VALLEY BELOW. DAWG WAS ON A STAKEOUT A COUPLE MILES AWAY, AND FOLLOWED THE DISTRESS CALL TO THE FRENZIED CANINE. THE STUBBORN KNOTS, ALONG WITH DAISY'S ANIMATED JUBILATION, MADE RELEASING HER DIFFICULT.

"I KNOW YER APPRECIATIVE," DAWG BARKED WITH EXASPERATION, "BUT THIS WOULD GO A LOT QUICKER IF YA'D STOP LICKIN' MY FACE."

DAWG DROVE DAISY HOME, THEN TOOK OFF TO TRACK DOWN THE THREE THUGS AND BRING THEM TO JUSTICE.

AFTER HER DEVASTATING EPISODE, DAISY EXPERIENCED PTSD (POST–TYING STRESS DISORDER). WHEN SHE WASN'T LAYING ON THE COUCH WATCHING TV AND EATING JUNK DOG FOOD, DAISY WOULD EXHIBIT DESTRUCTIVE BEHAVIOR INCLUDING OBSESSIVE LICKING,

TEARING UP NEWSPAPERS, AND STEALING SHOES. SHE WAS TRAPPED IN A WHINE-BARK PATTERN. THE FEW TIMES DAISY APPEARED IN PUBLIC, SHE WAS PARANOID, CONSTANTLY LOOKING OVER HER HINDQUARTERS. WOOLLY FINALLY CONVINCED HER TO GET BACK INTO THERAPY.

Depressed Daisy

DR. MCGROWL CAME TO DAISY'S HOME, AND SHE TOLD HIM ABOUT HER DOGNAPPING EXPERIENCE.

"I FEEL VIOLATED," DAISY WHIMPERED. "I BADLY WANT TO BITE SOMEONE."

DR. MCGROWL GENTLY ARFED, "RETALIATION IS NOT THE ANSWER. LET SLEEPING DOGS LIE."

"BUT I CAN'T FORGET IT," DAISY WHINED. "I CAN'T JUST ROLL OVER AND PLAY DUMB."

DR. MCGROWL HAD NO CHOICE BUT TO USE HIS SIGNATURE TOUGH-LOVE TACTIC: "DAISY, IF YOU CAN'T RUN WITH THE BIG DOGS, STAY ON THE PORCH!" DAISY'S WEEPY EYES LIT UP FOR THE FIRST TIME IN MONTHS. "EVERY DOG HAS ITS DAY," HE ADDED, "AND THIS IS YOURS." DR. MCGROWL AGGRESSIVELY BARKED, "YOU HAVE A BIG DOG PERSONALITY IN A SMALL DOG BODY. NOW GET OUT THERE AND SHOW 'EM WHAT YOU'RE MADE OF!"

IT WORKED! DAISY WAS NOW BACK ON TRACK FOR THE FIRST PART OF THE WORLD'S MOST SPECTACULAR DOG COMPETITION: *PROJECT DOG RUN.*

Leg IV

Part 1

Project Dog Run

Sewing a Frock for the Fashion-Challenged

FROM THE MOMENT SHE STEPPED INTO THE
NEW YORK CITY LOCATION OF *PROJECT DOG
RUN*, THE FIRST OF THREE COMPETITIONS
SHE WOULD NEED TO WIN TO BE NAMED THE
WORLD'S MOST SPECTACULAR DOG, DAISY
FELT AT HOME. SHE COULD RELATE TO THE
CREATIVELY APPOINTED CANINES SPORTING

EVERYTHING FROM SNOUT RINGS TO FULL—BODY TATTOOS AND PSYCHEDELIC STREAKED MOHAWK HAIRCUTS. SOME CONTESTANTS WORKED WITH SEWING MACHINES THAT WERE SET AGAINST A BACKDROP OF EXOTIC BOLTS OF FABRIC AND COLORFUL SPOOLS OF THREAD; OTHERS BUSILY ALTERED OUTFITS HANGING ON DRESS FORMS, HOLDING STRAIGHT PINS IN THEIR TEETH.

INTRODUCTIONS WERE MADE BY MENTOR TIM RUN, A GENIAL GOLDEN RETRIEVER: COTTON CANDY, DETROIT, CHRISTYN, WEDNESDAY, SANTORINI, JARFEREE, AND DAISY'S *AMERICAN HOWLER* COMPETITOR, JADE, WERE THE OTHER CONTESTANTS.

TIM BARKED, "GATHER 'ROUND, EVERYONE. FOR YOUR FIRST ELIMINATION ASSIGNMENT, YOU WILL HIT THE STREETS OF NEW YORK TO FIND FASHION—CHALLENGED SOULS. YOU'LL BE CREATING A WHOLE NEW LOOK FOR THEM, AND THEY WILL WEAR YOUR CLOTHING ON THE RUNWAY TO BE JUDGED BY OUR PANEL OF ICONIC FASHION DESIGNERS...LOSERS WILL GO HOME. NOW CARRY ON AND MAKE IT WORK!"

THE LAST THING ANY CONTESTANT WANTED WAS FOR HEIDI, THE BEAUTIFUL WEIMARANER AND MODEL/HOST OF THE PROGRAM, TO GIVE TWO QUICK LICKS ON EACH CHEEK AND YIP, "ARF WIEDERSEHEN."

Cover GRRRL Model/Host, Heidi

WEDNESDAY, THE BOSTON TERRIER, WAS THE FIRST TO FALL. HER DESIGN, A WHITE RUFFLED PANTALOON OUTFIT WITH TINY RED SOCKS EMBROIDERED ON THE PINSTRIPED BODICE, WAS TOPPED OFF WITH A RHINESTONE-EMBELLISHED BOSTON RED SOX BASEBALL CAP. WEDNESDAY

DIDN'T FORESEE THE EXPLOSIVE ANGER SUCH A BLATANT POLITICALLY INCORRECT STATEMENT WOULD CAUSE IN NEW YORK.

DAISY WON THE FIRST CHALLENGE. THE CONSERVATIVE BLACK PANTS SUIT SHE CREATED FOR HER FASHION-CHALLENGED SUBJECT, A SQUAT, MIDDLE-AGED BULLDOG NAMED GERTRUDE GLOTZ, HAD AN INNOVATIVE FEATURE. HIDDEN ZIPPERS ON EACH LEG ALLOWED THE PANTS TO EASILY CHANGE INTO AN ELEGANT SKIRT. THE REVERSIBLE DAYTIME JACKET CHANGED INTO A GLITTERY OFF-THE-SHOULDER EVENING FROCK. "G G" WAS "GOING GLAM," THANKS TO DAISY.

ONE-BY-ONE, THE COMPETITORS FELL BY THE WAYSIDE AS DAISY SURVIVED CHALLENGE AFTER CHALLENGE — THE MOST DIFFICULT BEING "GIVE MILEY CYPRUS AN AGE-APPROPRIATE LOOK."

IN THE END, THERE WERE ONLY TWO DOGS STANDING...DAISY, AND CHRISTYN, AN ANNOYING YORKSHIRE TERRIER. WHILE DESIGNING IN THE WORKROOM, CHRISTYN WOULD FIDGET, PACING BACK AND FORTH. "OHMIGOSH, OHMIGOSH, I NEED TO HURRY,

hurry, hurry. There's not enough time," he'd bark over and over.

For the final challenge, Tim ushered in an unruly pack of dogs. There was a lot of growling and snapping until Tim barked, "Speak softly to me."

Daisy's eyes bugged out when she realized she was face-to-face with the cast members of the Reality show, *Jersey Shack*. Their lifestyles and fashion sense were off the reality charts and now Tim was telling her she had to design clothing for their program's next season.

A tough-looking Italian Spritz named "Snarki" was constantly making calls on her cell phone while twirling her fur with her forepaw. She had a spray-on tan, threaded eyebrows, big teased hair with a poof in the back, and a garish low-cut tie-dyed T-shirt with a leopard print skirt. And she wore enough makeup for an entire kennel. Daisy was intently studying her, trying to get a handle on a design, when Snarki snapped

AT HER, "WHATCHA LOOKIN' AT? AIN'T YOUSE EV-A SEEN A GOIL FROM JOISEY B'FORE?"

DAISY LOWERED HER EARS AND BACKED AWAY, TURNING TO SEVERAL OTHER MEMBERS OF THE CAST — THE ITALIAN GREYHOUND, "PAULYDOG," WHO WAS STANDING IN FRONT OF THE MIRROR, APPLYING TONS OF GEL ON HIS BLOWOUT HAIRDO, AND A MALTESE, JENNA "J BOWWOW," WEARING A SHOCKING YELLOW TANK WITH A PLUNGING NECKLINE AND POLKA-DOT MINI-SHORTS WHICH SHE'D BOUGHT AT HEINRICH'S OF HOLLYWOOD. CHRISTYN WAS BUZZING ABOUT, CHATTERING NERVOUSLY AND MAKING SKETCHES. HE JUST HAD TO RUN OVER TO DAISY AND TELL HER THAT SNARKI HAD BEEN ARFING SMACK ABOUT HER TO PAULY AND JENNA.

A STRIKING ITALIAN MASTIFF, IKE "THE SOLUTION" SALIVATINO ARRIVED WITH FREE WEIGHTS IN HIS PAWS. WHAT A HUNK, DAISY THOUGHT, NOTICING HIS IMPRESSIVE ABS. IKE NODDED TO THE TWO CONTESTANTS, THEN LEFT, FIST-PUMPING HIS FRIENDS AND WOOFING, "HEY, GOTTA' GTL, BRO" ON THE WAY OUT.

THE TWO FINALISTS WENT BACK TO THEIR

HOMES FOR A WEEK TO CREATE THEIR COLLECTIONS FOR THE FOUR STARS OF THE SHOW. DAISY CALLED HERS "THE ON-TREND SEASIDE HEIGHTS COUTURE COLLECTION," FUN, ICE-CREAM-COLORED RIPPED COTTON FASHIONS AND IRIDESCENT T-SHIRTS FOR THE BEACH, BOARDWALK, GYM, AND BARS.

CHRISTYN JUST DIDN'T UNDERSTAND THE CULTURE OF *JERSEY SHACK*. HE OFFERED ORANGE GRECIAN GOWNS FOR THE LADIES AND PLAID BATHING SUITS FOR THE GENTS. CHRISTYN'S COLLECTION "SOPHISTICATION AT THE BURGER JOINT" WAS A FLOP. DAISY WON *PROJECT DOG RUN*, AND ADVANCED TO THE NEXT CHALLENGE.

Leg IV

Part 2

Top Mutt Chef

Chef Daisy and Her Signature Dish,
All-American Dogs Served Eight Ways

Daisy barely had a chance to catch her breath before it was time to leave for Paris, the location of the second phase of The *World's Most Spectacular Dog* competition, *Top Mutt Chef*. She dug into her trunk, retrieved her lucky beret, and boarded the plane.

A FIELD OF TWENTY CANINES FROM AROUND THE GLOBE WERE GATHERED AND QUICKLY PARED DOWN TO TEN AFTER A VOLLEY OF WRITTEN TESTS, INTERVIEWS, AND AN INITIAL CHALLENGE DIRECTED BY CHEF ANTSY, THE IMPOSING GORDON SETTER AND OWNER OF THE FAMOUS LONDON RESTAURANT, THE SAVORY BEEFCHEWER.

AT THE END OF A GRUELING WEEK, THE CANINES WERE USHERED INTO THE KITCHEN OF A CULINARY INSTITUTE WHERE CHEF ANTSY STOOD BEFORE THEM, PAWS ON HIS HIPS. HE WAS NOT PLEASED. "WHERE HAVE YOU BEEN? THIS IS NOT DISNEYLAND. WE ARE ON A SCHEDULE," HE YELPED. THE ASSIGNMENT FOR CHEF ANTSY AND HIS NEW ASSISTANT CHEFS WAS TO PUT ON A DINNER PARTY FOR 500 PATRONS OF THE LOUVRE, WITH THE THEME, "GAME CUISINE PAIRED WITH HUNTING ART."

AMIDST A BARRAGE OF ORDERS BARKED OUT BY CHEF ANTSY, THE KITCHEN BECAME A BEEHIVE OF ACTIVITY AS THE CHEFS RUSHED ABOUT, GRABBING POTS AND PANS FROM SHELVES, CHOPPING VEGETABLES, FILLETING

FISH, CARVING MEATS, AND SAUTÉING FOOD ON THE STOVES. SOME CONTESTANT CHEFS MADE PETTY MISTAKES THAT RAISED THE IRE OF CHEF ANTSY, AND WERE SENT HOME RIGHT ON THE SPOT. CECIL, THE MINIATURE PINSCHER, MADE AN UNFORGIVABLE ERROR. HE BROKE GOOSE EGGS OVER CHEF'S SIGNATURE DISH, *BRAISED WOODCOCK-STUFFED PHEASANT WITH GOOSEBERRY FOIS GRAS REDUCTION TOPPED BY POACHED QUAIL EGGS.* "HOW COULD YOU BE SO DOGGONE STUPID?" CHEF SCREAMED, THE FUR RISING ON HIS BACK. "A GOOSE EGG FOR YOU!" HE ADDED, MAKING A BIG ZERO WITH HIS PAW. "NOW GET LOST, DOG!" HE SCREECHED, POINTING AT THE DOOR.

PEDRO, THE CHIHUAHUA, COMMITTED AN UNPARDONABLE SIN WHEN HE WAS CAUGHT LICKING DIRECTLY FROM THE POT OF HASENPFEFFER STEW. DAISY LOWERED HER EARS IN ANTICIPATION OF THE HIGH-PITCHED GROWLS THAT SHE KNEW WOULD BE ENSUING BETWEEN THE TWO CANINES. PEDRO LUNGED AT CHEF, YAPPING IN FRUSTRATION. CHEF ANTSY HARSHLY PUT HIM DOWN IN FRONT OF THE OTHER CHEFS, AND PEDRO LEFT IN DISGRACE.

DAISY STAYED UNDER THE RADAR, OFFERING HER ASSISTANCE TO ANTSY IN ANY WAY NEEDED. "CHEF, MAY I ADD SOME HERBS TO MY SAUCE TO SUIT YOUR TASTE? DO YOU WANT ME TO RUN OUT AND BUY MORE BAGUETTES?" SHE ARFED. AND SHE WAS ALWAYS DOING WITHOUT BEING ASKED.

DAISY WAS REWARDED WITH A PLACE IN THE FINALS ALONG WITH BERTHA, AN OLD ENGLISH SHEEPDOG, JACQUES, A FRENCH BULLDOG, CHIN, A CHINESE CRESTED HAIRLESS, AND EVA, A HUNGARIAN VIZSLA. THE CHALLENGE WAS TO CREATE A SEVEN-COURSE MEAL ATOP THE EIFFEL TOWER. THE JUDGES INCLUDED SEVERAL FOOD CRITICS AND CHEFS WOLFHOUND PUCK, ERIC NIPPER, BO 'BELLY-BUSTING' BERNARDINO, AND PAWDRA LEAN. THE SAINT BERNARD, CHEF BO, WAS CHOSEN FOR THE PANEL FOLLOWING HIS METEORIC RISE FROM HOLLYWOOD NIGHTCLUB BOUNCER TO HOTSHOT CHEF. CHEF LEAN, A GOLDENDOODLE, WAS THERE BECAUSE OF HER RECENT CULINARY EPIPHANY AFTER A VISIT TO GREECE, WHEN SHE VOWED TO MAKE HUGE CHANGES IN HER COOKING BY SUBSTITUTING OLIVE OIL FOR BUTTER IN ALL HER RECIPES.

After food preparation, the canines presented their cuisine to the judges. A tiny bite-sized morsel was offered by each contestant chef before the first course. It didn't impress Chef Bo, as he inhaled each one and complained, "You've got to be kidding! There's not enough food here to feed a hummingbird."

When the appetizer and salad courses arrived, all but Daisy presented small platings, the newest trend. Chef Bo didn't even wait for the chefs' statements and descriptions of the dishes — he pounced on the food and licked the plates clean, ending each dish with a loud burp. He was also constantly referring to his fellow judges as cooks instead of chefs. This type of boorish behavior was never before seen in the sophisticated world of haute cuisine, and it caused quite a stir at the judges' table.

Chef Bo's stomach was still growling, but Daisy saved the day when she brought out her meat entree, *All-American Dogs Served Eight Ways*. She'd combined Maine

RED SNAPPERS, NEW JERSEY RIPPERS, DIXIE DOGS, RHODE ISLAND GAGGAHS, D.C. HALF-SMOKES, SONORAN WIENERS, CHICAGO RED HOTS, AND NEW YORK CONEYS TO CREATE AN EXPLOSION OF FLAVORS...FULL-BODIED PORTIONS, SERVED ON THREE-FOOT DIAMETER PLATTERS.

"BRAVO," BARKED CHEF BO, HIS EYES GROWING PRACTICALLY AS WIDE AS THE PLATTERS. THE OTHER JUDGES AGREED AND WAVED OFF THE OTHER ENTREES EVEN BEFORE THEY ARRIVED. DAISY'S COMPETITORS WERE TOLD, "PACK YOUR FOOD BOWLS AND LEAVE," AND IT WAS UNANIMOUS: THE *TOP MUTT CHEF* TITLE WENT TO DAISY.

Leg IV

Part 3

Retriever

The Castaways
ArfinBarkin and GnawboneTribes

ONE WEEK LATER...

DAISY WAS IN A DEEP SLEEP ON A PLANE HEADED TO THE LAST LEG OF THE *WORLD'S MOST SPECTACULAR DOG* COMPETITION — THE GRANDDADDY OF ALL REALITY SHOWS, *RETRIEVER.* THE PRODUCTION COMPANY WAS SHORT ON MONEY; INSTEAD OF A REMOTE

TROPICAL PARADISE IN THE MALDIVES, THE
CASTAWAYS WERE BEING MAROONED ON AN
ISLAND OFF THE COAST OF NEW JERSEY.

THE SMALL CANINE WAS PHYSICALLY
EXHAUSTED FROM THE ARDUOUS SCHEDULE SHE'D
BEEN KEEPING, AND WAS ALSO UNDER MENTAL
DURESS ON LEARNING THE TEN CONTESTANTS
WERE GOING TO BE DROPPED OFFSHORE BY
PARACHUTE.

DAISY HAD AN OBSESSIVE FEAR OF GETTING
WET AND DIDN'T KNOW HOW TO SWIM BEYOND
A WEAK DOGGY-PADDLE. SHE WAS GRATEFUL
FOR ONE THING...EACH DOG WAS ALLOWED TO
BRING ONE PERSONAL ITEM, AND DAISY'S
CHOICE WAS A PAIR OF KIDDIE WATER WINGS.
THE "DROP" WOULDN'T TRAUMATIZE HER TOO
MUCH.

IN ORDER TO BE NAMED "LONE RETRIEVER,"
SHE'D HAVE TO "OUTFOX, OUTBARK, AND
OUTBEG" THE COMPETITION, AND THIS WAS
A FORMIDABLE GROUP OF HOUNDS. DAISY HAD
GOOD CAUSE TO BE CONCERNED. MANY OF HER
OPPONENTS WERE LARGE WATER DOGS WITH
LOTS OF STAMINA AND HAD A LIFETIME OF
EXPERIENCE IN RETRIEVING.

AFTER THE *ArfinBarkin* AND *Gnawbone* TRIBES WERE NAMED, ALLIANCES WERE FORMED. DAISY ATTRACTED AN UNLIKELY FRIEND IN *ArfinBarkin*, BOSTON TERRIER ROB. ALL DAY LONG HE LOUNGED IN THE HAMMOCK INSTEAD OF HELPING AROUND CAMP, CONSTANTLY WHINING, "IT'S TOO HOT HERE AND THE SAND FLEAS ARE A-BITIN'!" DAISY TRIED TO GET HIM TO DO SOME WORK BY POKING HIM WITH HER COLD NOSE, BUT ROB COULDN'T BE MOVED — HE'D JUST ROLL OVER AND ARF, "MY DOGS ARE BARKIN'."

DAISY KNEW SHE'D HAVE TO LEAVE HER TRUSTING DEMEANOR BEHIND AND PLAY THE GAME, BUT DIDN'T WANT TO SACRIFICE HER INTEGRITY IN DOING SO. AS THE GROUP OF CASTAWAYS IN HER *ArfinBarkin* TRIBE WERE SLOWLY ELIMINATED, SHE BECAME INCREASINGLY WARY OF A REMAINING TRIBEMATE, JOHNNY FOULPLAY, A HAIRLESS CHIHUAHUA. JOHNNY PLAYED THE GAME WITH HYENA-LIKE STRATEGY.

Gnawbone WAS LOSING CHALLENGE AFTER CHALLENGE INCLUDING THE "TAIL-CHASING SPRINT", "SQUEAKER-TOY TUG", "DANGLING

SAUSAGE LEAP", AND "FUR BALL FROLIC". THE ONLY *GNAWBONE* CONTESTANT WHO POSED A THREAT WAS RICHARD FETCH, AN UNABASHED OTTER HOUND. HE HAD AN ANNOYING HABIT OF PARADING AROUND AU NATURAL; BUT HE WAS RESOURCEFUL, AND CONTINUALLY DISARMED HIS OPPONENTS WITH HIS OUTRAGEOUS BEHAVIOR. AFTER EVERY TRIBAL COUNCIL, HE WOULD STAY, PUMPING HIS PAWS AND BARKING OUT, "I GOT GAME!" MEANWHILE, ANOTHER CANINE SADLY LEFT, HIS OR HER TIKI TORCH EXTINGUISHED, AS THE REALITY SHOW'S HOST, JEFF PUG, PROCLAIMED, "THE TRIBE HAS BARKED!"

THE NIGHT BEFORE FINAL TRIBAL COUNCIL, THE FINAL FOUR CONTESTANTS, DAISY, ROB, RICHARD, AND JOHNNY, ENGAGED IN A LOT OF WHISPER—BARK AS THEY DISCUSSED THEIR STRATEGIES AND REFLECTED UPON THEIR *RETRIEVER* EXPERIENCES. THE NEXT MORNING THEY WOULD COMPETE IN THE FINAL CHALLENGE, "OUTDIG". THREE IMMUNITY IDOLS WERE BURIED DEEP IN THE SAND ON THE BEACH. TWO WERE MADE OF WORTHLESS BONE AND THE ONLY ONE THAT COUNTED WAS GLASS CRYSTAL.

At daybreak, when members of Tribal Council arfed "Go," the four hounds took off like a shot and raced to various beach areas marked by flags, which were clues to where the crystal idol might be buried, and each started to furiously dig. Every so often, Johnny Foulplay would scamper over and nip at Daisy and Rob's heels until Jeff Pug called him off. Johnny was soon eliminated for bad dog behavior. Richard tried to deter Daisy and Rob by "accidentally" kicking sand in their faces, but that only made the duo more determined.

Daisy was the lucky dog. She saw the tip of the crystal idol at the bottom of her four foot deep hole. But before she could unearth it, she was distracted by a faint yelping out in the ocean. Daisy stood on her hind legs to look. About 100 yards offshore, three puppies were struggling to climb onto a plank. Even though immunity was hers for the taking, plus her fear of water, Daisy knew what she had to do.

MOMENTS LATER SHE HAD DOG-PADDLED OUT TO THE PUPS, AND NOSED THEM UP ONTO THE PLANK. SHE REMOVED HER RETRIEVER HEADBAND, SLIPPED IT OVER ONE END OF THE WOOD, GRABBED THE FABRIC WITH HER TEETH, AND PULLED IT BACK TO SHORE. THE MANGY SHIVERING PUPS TOLD DAISY THAT GUS, THE PUPPY FARM OWNER, USED THAT AREA TO DUMP DEAD-END DOGS.

DAISY LOOKED UP THE BEACH AND, TO HER DISMAY, RICHARD FETCH WAS STANDING IN HER HOLE, TRIUMPHANTLY RAISING THE CRYSTAL TROPHY OVER HIS HEAD. DAISY WAS SO INFURIATED THAT RICHARD HAD WON IN SUCH AN UNDER-PAWED WAY, SHE HEAVED HER CHEST AND LET OUT A HEART-WRENCHING CRY. THE CASTAWAYS AND CREW HAD TO COVER THEIR EARS AS THE SHRILL DOUBLE-OCTAVE HIGH "A" NOTE PIERCED THE AIR. BUT NONE WERE MORE SHOCKED THAN RICHARD FETCH, WHEN BOTH THE GLASS AND HIS HOPES FOR IMMUNITY WERE SHATTERED.

HER PUPPY RESCUE HAD DISQUALIFIED DAISY, AND THE FINAL VOTE FROM TRIBAL COUNCIL CAME DOWN TO ROB AND RICHARD. THE JURY

UNANIMOUSLY THREW THE BONE TO BOSTON TERRIER ROB, BESTOWING HIM THE TITLE, "LONE RETRIEVER." BUT DAISY COULDN'T HAVE CARED LESS THAT SHE'D LOST THE *WORLD'S MOST SPECTACULAR DOG* COMPETITION BY A HAIR. THROUGH HER EXPERIENCE ON THAT NEW JERSEY ISLAND, DAISY DISCOVERED SOMETHING MUCH MORE REWARDING THAN A TITLE. SHE FOUND HER LIFE'S MISSION.

Leg IV

Part 4

A New Leash On Life

**Glam Daisy Walking the Red Carpet at
the Acadogmy Awards**

Daisy may not have been best in the show, but she finally understood the true meaning of "a dog's life." Daisy was now committed to using her wealth and

NOTORIETY TO HELP DOGMANITY. SHE CREATED SEVERAL CANINE FOUNDATIONS THROUGH HER PHILANTHROPIC VENTURES. *GOLDEN YEARS DOGHOUSING* BUILT RETIREMENT HOMES ACROSS THE COUNTRY THAT ALLOWED ELDER CANINES TO LIVE THEIR SENIOR YEARS WITH DIGNITY, DECORUM, AND PURPOSE. *MUTT NO MORE* MOVED SHELTER DOGS OUT OF THEIR CONFINEMENT AND TRAINED THEM TO BE MODEL DOGIZENS. DAISY RECRUITED THE BULLDOG/POMERANIAN MIX REAL ESTATE MOGUL DONALD JUMP, TO BE THEIR MENTOR. THE DON-DOG, AS HE WAS NICKNAMED, HAD TO BE FREQUENTLY MONITORED BY DAISY BECAUSE OF HIS CONTROL ISSUES AND WOULD FREQUENTLY FIRE THE HELP. IN THE END HE GRACIOUSLY ACCEPTED DAISY'S ADVICE AND CRITICISM. THEREAFTER, HE TOOK GREAT SATISFACTION IN FINDING MEANINGFUL JOBS FOR THESE DOWN AND OUT DOGS, BARKING WITH ENTHUSIASM, "YOU'RE HIRED!" OTHER PROGRAMS STARTED BY DAISY INCLUDED *DOGS HELPING CATS*, WHICH GOT KITTIES OFF THE STREETS AND INTO LOVING DOGHOUSES. THE MUCH-HERALDED ORGANIZATION ALSO ENABLED YOUNGER CANINES AND FELINES

TO WORK FOR LODGING, MEALS AND HEALTH CARE BY TAKING ON SUCH WORK AS POOPER-SCOOPER DUTY, AND LICKING ENVELOPES FOR PHILANTHROPIC CAUSES.

ALTHOUGH DAISY WAS BUSIER THAN A ONE-EYED CAT WATCHING TWO MOUSE HOLES, SHE SAID YES WHEN OFFERED HER OWN BARK SHOW, *THE RANT AND PANT SHOW*, ON THE FOX TERRIER NETWORK AS A FORUM FOR YAPS AND MEOWS TO BE HEARD. THE FIRST THING SHE DID WAS REPLACE THE BLONDE-FURRED GLAMOUR PUPS APPEARING ON THE NEWS SEGMENT OF HER PROGRAM WITH SEASONED JOURNALISTS. DAISY'S REGULAR GUESTS INCLUDED NEWS PERSONALITIES HUSH DIMGROWL, RACHEL MADDOG, GLEN BARK, AND BILL MAUL. OTHER GUESTS WERE OFTEN INSERTED INTO THE MIX, WHICH ADDED A LOT MORE TEETH-BARING AND SNAPPING. DAISY LOVED TO GATHER CONTROVERSIAL GROUPS AND STAGE GOOD OLD-FASHIONED SNARLDOWNS, EVEN THOUGH HER GUESTS OFTEN FOUGHT LIKE, YOU GUESSED IT, CATS AND DOGS. THE MOST MEMORABLE CONFRONTATION WAS A BARKFEST BETWEEN TWO POLITICIANS...THE FEISTY ALASKAN HUSKY, SARAH GROWLIN',

AND A LITTLE BARKER NAMED ELIZABETH, A
DOUR CANARIAN WARREN HOUND.

Boston Terrier Rob

BUT DAISY GOT HER BIGGEST THRILL AND
SENSE OF ACCOMPLISHMENT THE DAY SHE

BOUGHT OUT Mr. Rufus AND TURNED HIS BED & BISCUIT INTO A HAPPY PUPPY FARM AND MUSIC SCHOOL; APPOINTING Woolly AS HEADMASTER. BOSTON TERRIER Rob WAS RESPONSIBLE FOR MAKING SURE ALL THE GUESTS GOT IN THEIR DOG NAPS AND WAS ALSO THE Holiday EVENT COORDINATOR.

Mary Bite AND Leashley, THE Wholesome TWINS, WERE PART OF THE STAFF AND LECTURED PUPPIES ON HOW TO GROW UP TO BE RESPONSIBLE AND RESPECTFUL ADULT DOGS.

Mary Bite and Leashley, The Wholesome Twins

CODY, THE TALENT AGENT WHO DISCOVERED DAISY, WAS A REGULAR AT THE INN AND WOULD FREQUENTLY BRING ASPIRING VOCALISTS ALONG TO ATTEND THE MUSIC SCHOOL. AS FOR GUS, HIS DOG DUMPING DAYS WERE OVER. HE WAS ARRESTED FOR CRUELTY TO ANIMALS AND SENTENCED TO A LONG STAY IN THE DOG PEN.

EVEN THOUGH DAISY LEFT THE GLITZ AND GLAMOUR OF HOLLYWOOD TO LIVE HER QUIET LIFE IN THE COUNTRY, SHE WAS NOT FORGOTTEN BY THE MANY FRIENDS SHE MADE THERE. WHEN DAISY WAS 50 IN DOG YEARS, SHE WALKED THE RED CARPET AT AN ACADOGMY AWARDS CEREMONY WHERE SHE WAS PRESENTED WITH A LIFETIME ACHIEVEMENT AWARD AND THE COVETED WHISKER STATUETTE. SHE HAD TEARS IN HER EYES AS SHE APPROACHED THE PODIUM AND WATCHED THE BIG SCREEN, FEATURING ELDERLY CANINES WITH CANES FILING EN MASSE THROUGH THE DOORS OF ONE OF HER RETIREMENT HOMES. IN ADDITION TO THIS HONOR, AMERICA'S SWEETHEART'S PAW PRINT WAS PLACED ON THE HOLLYWOOD LOPE OF FAME.

Hollywood Goes To The Dogs

DAISY HAD MORE EXPERIENCES THAN HER CAT FRIENDS HAD LIVES. BUT NOTHING GAVE HER AS MUCH JOY AS BEING ABLE TO LIVE HER SENIOR YEARS FULLY COMMITTED TO HELPING EVERY LOST DOG SHE POSSIBLY COULD. ON A TYPICAL DAY, SHE COULD BE SEEN OUT AND ABOUT LOOKING FOR YET ANOTHER LITTER TO ADOPT. PRETTY SOON DAISY HAD MORE PUPS THAN ANGELINA COLLIE AND BRAD PITBULL.

The Tail End

DEDICATION

To the "real Daisy" & her canine and feline friends.

Special thanks to Daisy's loyal pal, Woolly.

ABOUT THE AUTHOR:

Carol Wallace began her professional career as a fine artist represented by galleries in Bucks County, Pennsylvania, Litchfield County, Connecticut, the Massachusetts Berkshires, and Charlotte, North Carolina. Through the years she added commission artist, illustrator, writer, photographer, preservationist and published author to her list of accomplishments. Carol recently began licensing selected work to publishing companies and manufacturers of decorative giftware and fashion accessories.

Daisy's Reality Show Adventure is Carol's first book that she wrote and illustrated as an adjunct to her national Preserve America, a combination of fine art, photography, writing, and commerce. The goal and its associated Gatekeepers of History, which she founded in 1997, is to preserve the history, culture and tradition of Americana in multiple ways. The artist has traveled to every state in the U.S., working with members from the private and public sectors on this movement. Through her work of both a serious and humorous nature, Carol is dedicated to making a difference.

Carol's satirical novella is a fun study of American popular culture, the Reality show phenomenon and Hollywood, as well as commentary on the present political landscape. The protagonist she chose to present this allegory is a feisty Rat Terrier, the beloved dog of Carol's late father, a World War II veteran and member of the Greatest Generation. The "real Daisy" is now in her late 90s (in dog years), living with family on a cattle ranch in Montana. The book, reviewed as a "real tailwagger," was launched in Hollywood, California at Pink's Hot Dog Stand and was also selected for inclusion in Hollywood celebrity gift bags.

Carol Wallace resides in northwestern Connecticut at her country home with her husband, Rick. In addition to being an elected member of the Society of Illustrators, Salmagundi Art Club, and National League of American Pen Women, Carol is a Coast Guard Artist. She is listed in Who's Who in American Art.

Acknowledgments

I thank my husband, Rick; children, Rick, Jr. and Christy, Christine and Jeff; grandchildren, Britta, Theodore, Jack, and Henry; and other family and friends for their unwavering encouragement and support...you know who you are. I'm grateful to my Mom and Dad, who helped me to develop my creativity at an early age; and I appreciate the inspirational stories related to me by Daisy and Woolly's human family members, Doris, Mary, and Joe.

Thanks to my creative associates:

Cliff Carle for sharing his expertise in humor writing and providing editorial advice.

Elaine Lanmon at Just Ink Digital Design and David Collins at Wingspan Press for the book conversion layout.

Renee Barrett for the cover design.

Richard Hubbard for his graphic art/Web promotion assistance and for his creation, the Ruly font featured in the book.

Greg O'Brien, for his Voice-over introducing Daisy's story on her Web site.

To hear a reading of Leg lll, The Dognapping, by Irish Setter, Greg O'Brien, go to: DaisyDogEnterprises.com/sample.htm

Filmmaker Michael "Puggy" Pugnose, featured in The Dognapping audio.

www.ingramcontent.com/pod-product-compliance
Lightning Source LLC
Chambersburg PA
CBHW042043190626
46815CB00020B/2